The Case That Haunted Me:

A Psychological Thriller

By

Richard Trillion Mantey

Table of Contents

Dedication

This book is dedicated to those who carry invisible stories.

To the ones who smile while silently fighting battles no one can see…

To the ones haunted not by what happened—but by what was never understood…

And to those who search for truth, even when it hurts.

May you find clarity in the chaos…

And strength in what once tried to break you.

Acknowledgments

Every story is never written alone.

I want to express my deepest gratitude to those who believe in the power of storytelling—not just as entertainment, but as a force that can heal, awaken, and transform.

To the readers—thank you for your trust. For allowing these words into your mind, your emotions, and your time. Your curiosity and imagination give life to every page.

To the thinkers, observers, and truth-seekers—your questions about human nature, memory, and reality continue to inspire stories like this one.

To those who have experienced moments that linger… memories that echo… and truths that refuse to stay buried—this story exists because of you.

And finally, to the unseen forces that shape every story—intuition, emotion, and the quiet whispers of the mind—thank you for guiding this journey.

Chapter 1: The Case That Followed Me Home

The Night of the Incident

The night of the incident was shrouded in an unsettling silence, broken only by the distant rustle of leaves in the wind. It was a night that felt different, as if the air itself was pregnant with secrets waiting to be unveiled. In the small town of Willow Creek, where everyone knew each other's business, the atmosphere was thick with an unshakeable tension. Little did I know, this was the beginning of a haunting that would follow me home, entwining my life with the shadows of the past.

As I walked through the dimly lit streets, I couldn't shake the feeling that I was being watched. The streetlamps flickered, casting eerie shadows that danced along the pavement. Memories of the incident flooded my mind, the details playing out like a broken record. I recalled the frantic whispers of the townsfolk, each recounting their version of the events that transpired that fateful night, creating a tapestry of confusion and fear that would haunt me for years to come.

In the heart of it all was a mystery that seemed almost too tangled to unravel. The disappearance of Sarah Mitchell had sent shockwaves through Willow Creek, leaving an indelible mark on its residents. As I pieced together the moments leading up to her vanishing, I felt a strange compulsion to dive deeper into the investigation, despite the risks involved. The more I uncovered, the more I realized that the truth was far more sinister than I had ever imagined.

The nights were the hardest, filled with sleepless hours replaying the events in my mind, each detail sharpening the edge of my obsession. I found myself at the edge of the woods where Sarah was last seen, grappling with the same questions that had plagued the town for years. The moonlight filtered through the trees, illuminating the path that had been forever altered by tragedy. It was a reminder that some secrets are buried deep, yet they cling to the surface, refusing to fade away.

Ultimately, the night of the incident became a turning point in my life—a moment that would forever intertwine my fate with the haunting echoes of Willow Creek. As I delved deeper into the investigation, I became acutely aware that the case wasn't merely an unsolved mystery; it was a reflection of my own struggles, my own fears manifesting in the shadows of the past. The night had changed everything, and as the truth began to unravel, I realized that some cases never truly close, but instead, follow us home, lingering like a specter in the dark.

Shadows of the Past

The echoes of the past lingered in the quiet corners of the small town, where every shadow seemed to tell a story. As I walked down the familiar streets, memories flooded back, each one sharper than the last. These were not just recollections; they were fragments of a puzzle that had haunted me for years. The case that had once consumed my life now felt like a ghost, following me home, whispering secrets I was desperate to uncover.

In the dim light of my living room, I could almost see the faces of those affected by the tragedy that had unfolded years ago. Each unsolved mystery was a thread connecting me to them, weaving an intricate tapestry of grief and unresolved questions. I felt an unshakeable connection to the victims, their stories intertwined with my own journey of discovery. Was I merely an observer, or had I become a participant in this haunting narrative?

As I delved deeper into the old case files, I felt a chill run down my spine. The small-town secrets began to unravel, each revelation more chilling than the last. I was no longer just a sleuth; I was a vessel for their pain, driven by an insatiable need to bring closure not only to their families but also to myself. The shadows of the past were not merely memories; they were living entities, urging me to confront the truth.

Every late-night conversation with my partner in this investigation revealed layers of complexity I had never anticipated. The dynamic between us shifted as we uncovered hidden motives and buried truths that lay dormant for too long. It wasn't just about solving a case; it was about understanding the emotional landscape that surrounded it. The psychological toll weighed heavily on us both, but we pressed on, determined to bring light to the darkness that had enveloped our town.

In the end, I realized that the shadows of the past would always be a part of me. Each step closer to the truth brought a mix of exhilaration and dread, reminding me that some mysteries are best left unsolved. Yet, as I navigated through the remnants of that fateful night, I understood that uncovering the past was not just a quest for justice, but a journey toward healing—and perhaps, finally, peace.

Chapter 2: A Small Town's Secrets

Whispers in the Wind

The wind whispered secrets as Emma stepped into the old, forgotten town once more. Each gust carried with it the memories of her past, a haunting echo of the case that had once consumed her. The rustle of leaves felt like the sighs of those who had suffered, their stories woven into the fabric of this place. Emma's heart raced as she recalled the faces of the victims, their eyes pleading for justice, their stories still unfinished. She had promised them she would find the truth, but the shadows of the past loomed large, threatening to engulf her.

As she walked the familiar streets, she could almost hear the laughter of children playing, now replaced by an eerie silence. The quaint houses, once filled with warmth, stood as silent witnesses to the tragedies that had unfolded. Emma felt a chill run down her spine, the air thick with unspoken words and unresolved tensions. The townsfolk had their own secrets, and as she re-entered their lives, she could sense their unease. What had she awakened by returning? What had been buried beneath the surface?

Emma's instincts kicked in; she was not just a visitor but a part of this intricate web of intrigue. She sought out the local café, a hub of gossip and whispers, where the barista greeted her with a mix of recognition and suspicion. Over steaming cups of coffee, she began to piece together fragments of conversations, each one a thread leading her deeper into the mystery. The patrons spoke in hushed tones, their eyes darting around as if the walls themselves had ears. Emma knew she had to tread carefully; trust was a luxury she could not afford.

As night fell, the wind picked up, howling like a wounded animal. Emma felt an invisible presence following her, a reminder of the case that haunted her still. With every step, she could sense the weight of the past pressing down on her shoulders. The darkness seemed alive, wrapping around her like a shroud, whispering truths she had yet to uncover. She was driven by a need to confront her demons, to unravel the secrets that had clung to her like a second skin since her first investigation.

In the dead of night, she stood at the edge of the town, staring into the abyss of the woods that bordered it. The trees swayed ominously, their branches reaching out like skeletal fingers. Emma closed her eyes, letting the whispers of the wind guide her thoughts. She could feel the spirits of the past urging her forward, compelling her to take the final steps toward resolution. This was not just a case; it was her life, intertwined with the lives of those who had come before her, demanding closure in a world where the echoes of the past never truly fade away.

The Town's Dark History

The town of Eldridge had a veneer of charm that belied its darker undercurrents. Nestled among rolling hills and picturesque streets, the quaint houses and manicured gardens seemed to whisper secrets of a simpler time. Yet, beneath this façade lay a history stained with shadows, where echoes of unresolved mysteries lingered like specters. The townspeople knew better than to discuss the past openly, for fear of awakening the ghosts that haunted their lives, and perhaps, their very souls.

As a child, I had heard snippets of tales about the old mill at the edge of town, where strange occurrences had driven locals to abandon their livelihoods. The mill had once thrived, powered by the river that rushed nearby, but it had fallen silent after a series of tragic accidents. Whispers of disappearances and unexplained phenomena surrounded the site, making it a place of dread and intrigue. Even now, years later, the air felt thick with the weight of its haunted legacy, and I could not shake the sense that the past was not truly buried.

My investigation into the town's dark history felt personal. It was as if the unresolved mysteries were intertwining with my own life, pulling me deeper into a narrative I couldn't escape. Each interview with the townsfolk revealed layers of fear and reluctance to confront the truth. They spoke in hushed tones, their eyes darting nervously as they recounted events that shaped their lives. Through their stories, the lines between fact and folklore blurred, leaving me questioning what was real and what was merely a product of collective memory.

There was a particular tale that stood out—a story of a woman who had vanished without a trace, her absence felt by the entire community. As I delved deeper, I discovered that her disappearance was not an isolated incident but part of a disturbing pattern that hinted at a darker force at play. The more I unearthed, the more I realized that the town's past was not just a series of unfortunate events; it was a tapestry woven with secrets that connected generations, binding the present to the haunting shadows of yesterday.

As I stood at the old mill one fateful evening, the sun setting behind the hills, I felt a chill run down my spine. The air crackled with an energy that suggested I was not alone. The whispers of the past were closing in, and I was left with the unsettling realization that the town's dark history was not merely a backdrop to my investigation but a living entity that would follow me home, intertwining my fate with those who had vanished long ago.

Chapter 3: Reopening Old Wounds

The Letter That Changed Everything

The letter arrived on a dreary Tuesday, its envelope yellowed with age and the ink slightly smudged. As I held it in my trembling hands, a chill ran down my spine. The familiar scrawl belonged to someone I thought I had long left behind—a ghost of my past that had resurfaced to haunt me once more. It spoke of secrets buried deep within the heart of our small town, hints of a case that had never truly been solved. The words seemed to pulse with an energy that demanded my attention, pulling me back into a world I thought I had escaped.

Reading the letter felt like stepping into a time machine, taking me back to that fateful summer when everything changed. The memories flooded back with a vividness that was almost unbearable. I recalled the laughter of friends, the sunshine that bathed our sleepy streets, and the horrifying event that shattered our innocence. This letter was not just a message; it was a key, unlocking a door to old wounds that had yet to heal. I could feel the weight of unspoken truths pressing down on me, urging me to confront them.

As I delved deeper into the letter's content, I realized it was more than just a call to revisit the past; it was a compass guiding me toward a truth that had been concealed for too long. Each line was meticulously crafted, as if the writer had poured their very soul into the words. It hinted at connections I had overlooked, relationships that were more intertwined than I had ever imagined. The intricate web of family secrets and small-town dynamics began to unravel before my eyes, revealing a tapestry of betrayal and loyalty that was both disturbing and compelling.

I felt a surge of determination wash over me. This was my chance to reclaim my narrative, to take control of a story that had spiraled out of my grasp. I had spent years avoiding the shadows, but now they were beckoning me to return. With the letter as my guide, I resolved to confront those who had kept the truth hidden and to piece together the fragments of a mystery that had haunted me for far too long. The thrill of discovery pulsed through my veins, intertwining with a sense of dread that I could no longer ignore.

As I prepared to embark on this journey into the heart of darkness, I understood that this was not just about solving a case; it was about healing. The letter had changed everything, illuminating paths I never knew existed. I was ready to face the consequences of my past and to uncover the chilling truths that lay within. Each step forward would be a step toward redemption, not just for myself, but for the souls forever entwined with the case that had followed me home.

Gathering the Evidence

The air was thick with expectation as I stepped into the dimly lit room, a sense of urgency thrumming in my veins. Gathering the evidence was not just a task; it was a journey into the depths of my own psyche. Each photograph, each report, felt like a piece of my fractured past, beckoning me to confront what I had long tried to forget. I knew that the truth was buried beneath layers of denial and fear, and it was time to dig deep, to unearth the secrets that had haunted me for so long.

As I sifted through the files, the faces of those involved in the case stared back at me, their eyes filled with unspoken stories. I felt a connection to each soul, a thread weaving through time and pain, binding us together in this grim tapestry. The small town where it all began held its breath, harboring secrets that were as thick as the fog that rolled in each evening. It was a place where whispers could ignite a firestorm, where every shadow seemed to harbor a lingering presence.

I meticulously organized each piece of evidence, the mundane details transforming into a narrative that was both chilling and compelling. The patterns began to emerge, the connections revealing themselves like a long-forgotten melody. Memories flooded back, intertwining with the facts as I began to see the case not just as a puzzle to be solved but as a reflection of my own struggles and fears. My heart raced with the realization that what I was uncovering was not just about the crime; it was about me, about my own unresolved entanglements.

With every clue I followed, I felt a growing sense of connection to the victims and their families. Their stories became my own, and I could feel their pain echoing within me. Each twist and turn in the investigation drew me deeper into the emotional labyrinth that had ensnared us all. The ghosts of the past whispered in my ear, urging me to uncover the truth at any cost, to confront the shadows that had lingered for far too long.

As the pieces of the puzzle began to fit together, I realized that gathering the evidence was only the beginning. It was a catalyst for facing the deeper questions that haunted my heart. The case was not merely a mystery; it was a mirror reflecting my own fears and desires. I was no longer just an amateur sleuth but a participant in a story that transcended time and space, a tale of loss, redemption, and the relentless pursuit of truth.

Chapter 4: The Detective Duo

Partners in Crime

The small town of Willow Creek held its breath as the chilling news spread like wildfire: two seemingly innocent women, best friends since childhood, had been implicated in a series of unsolved crimes that haunted their community for decades. Days turned into weeks, and the whispers grew louder, echoing through the streets and alleyways. As the protagonist, I found myself drawn into their world, uncovering layers of secrets and lies that had festered beneath the surface for far too long. My heart raced with each new revelation, as I realized that the truth was far more twisted than I could have imagined.

In the heart of this psychological labyrinth lay the undeniable bond between the two women, a partnership forged in innocence but marred by the shadows of their past. Their friendship had been a sanctuary, a refuge from the harsh realities of life. Yet, as I dug deeper, I discovered that this camaraderie had transformed into a dangerous alliance, one that blurred the lines between loyalty and betrayal. The deeper I went into their history, the more I understood that their connection was not just about friendship; it was a lifeline tethering them to their darkest secrets.

What struck me most was the psychological entanglement I experienced as I navigated their story. I felt the weight of their guilt, the tug of their shared memories, and the fear that perhaps I too was becoming complicit in their crimes. I could not help but reflect on my own life, haunted by past decisions and the echoes of mistakes that lingered. This case was not just about solving a mystery; it was about confronting the ghosts that followed me home, a journey that left me questioning my own moral compass.

As I pieced together the puzzle, the stakes grew higher, and the danger became palpable. The town, once a picturesque backdrop, morphed into a character of its own, one that held its breath in anticipation of the inevitable confrontation. The nights were filled with anxiety, as I found myself pacing in the darkness, haunted by the faces of the women who had unwittingly become my partners in this unsettling dance. Their fates were intertwined with mine, and I felt the weight of their choices pressing down on my conscience.

In the end, the resolution of this intricate tale brought not just answers but an unsettling sense of closure. I had uncovered the truth behind their crimes, but at what cost? The journey left scars that would never fully heal, reminding me that in the world of psychological thrillers, the real crime often lies in the tangled web of human emotions. The case that haunted me was far from over;

it would linger in my thoughts, a constant reminder of the dark secrets that lay just beneath the surface, waiting to be unearthed once more.

Trust Issues

Trust issues can linger like shadows, obscuring the truth and complicating even the simplest interactions. For the protagonist, these feelings manifest in every relationship she holds dear, from friendships to romantic pursuits. Past betrayals haunt her, leaving a residue of doubt that colors her perceptions. Each glance, every spoken word, is dissected for hidden meanings, creating a chasm between her and those she longs to connect with.

As she delves deeper into the cold case that has gripped her small town, these trust issues become increasingly pronounced. The investigation stirs up not only the secrets of others but also her own buried fears. She grapples with the notion that perhaps the people closest to her are not who they seem. This inner turmoil becomes a backdrop to her sleuthing, as she questions the motives of everyone involved, including herself.

The small town setting amplifies her feelings of isolation. With every corner she turns, there are reminders of past relationships and haunting memories. The community, once a source of comfort, now feels like a trap filled with whispers and sidelong glances.

Each encounter is a reminder of how trust, once broken, can leave scars that take years to heal. The protagonist's determination to uncover the truth forces her to confront not just external mysteries but also the labyrinth of her own heart.

In this psychological battle, she finds unexpected allies and adversaries among the townsfolk. Some seem genuine, extending their hands in friendship, while others exude an air of suspicion. The protagonist must navigate this treacherous terrain, weighing her instincts against the desire for connection. What she learns about others will ultimately reflect back on her, challenging her to either close off further or embrace vulnerability once more.

As the case unfolds, the protagonist's journey reveals that trust is not merely given but earned, often through shared experiences and honesty. Each breakthrough in the investigation serves as a mirror, reflecting her own growth and the possibility of reconciliation with her past. The emotional stakes rise as she learns that to solve the case—and perhaps find peace—she must first confront the walls she has built around her heart.

Chapter 5: The Haunting Memories

Dreams That Disturb

In the dim light of her bedroom, Anna tossed and turned, her mind a whirlpool of unprocessed emotions and unresolved memories. Each night brought forth a new dream, vivid and unsettling, pulling her deeper into a past she thought she had buried. The figures in her dreams wore familiar faces, yet their expressions twisted in ways that haunted her waking hours. It felt as if they were trying to communicate something important, something she needed to uncover before it was too late.

These nocturnal disturbances weren't mere figments of her imagination; they were echoes of a case that had long haunted her small town. A young woman had vanished years ago, leaving behind a trail of questions that no one seemed eager to answer. As the dreams intensified, so did Anna's determination to dig deeper into the mystery. She could no longer ignore the signs that hinted at a connection between her past and the unresolved case; the dreams felt like a call to action.

One particularly vivid dream left her shaken to the core. In it, she stood in the town's abandoned park, the air thick with fog and a sense of foreboding. A voice whispered her name, urging her to follow. When she awoke, the lingering dread became an unshakable resolve. Anna knew she must confront the shadows of her past and the secrets that her dreams were so desperately trying to reveal.

As she delved into the investigation, Anna found herself piecing together not only the mystery of the missing woman but also the fragments of her own history. Each clue unearthed in her waking life tugged at her heartstrings, unraveling family secrets and long-buried traumas. Her dreams began to intertwine with her reality, blurring the lines between what was real and what was imagined. The deeper she went, the more she realized that the truth was not just about solving a case; it was about healing her own spirit.

Ultimately, Anna's journey through the dark corners of her dreams and the chilling reality of the cold case led her to a profound revelation. The haunting visions were not merely disturbances; they were a guide, leading her toward the understanding that sometimes, to confront the past, one must first embrace the discomfort it brings. As she stood at the crossroads of her dreams and reality, Anna felt empowered to reclaim her narrative, knowing that the shadows of the past would no longer dictate her future.

Voices from Beyond

The air was thick with anticipation as I walked through the old town, where whispers of the past mingled with the rustle of the leaves. Each creak of the wooden floorboards beneath my feet seemed to echo the stories long buried by time. I was no stranger to the weight of unresolved cases, but this one felt different. It was as if the very walls were alive, holding secrets that were eager to be unearthed. The lingering scent of lavender from the nearby fields reminded me of happier times, yet it only intensified the shadows of what had been lost.

As I delved deeper into the investigation, I discovered that the voices from beyond were not just figments of my imagination. They were the echoes of those who had suffered, their stories intertwined with my own. Each interview with the townsfolk revealed layers of fear and regret, painting a haunting picture of the events that led to the tragedy. Their haunted expressions spoke volumes, each one an invitation to peel back the layers of a mystery that had entwined itself around my heart like a vine.

Every detail I uncovered felt personal, as if the case were a mirror reflecting my own fears and desires. The more I learned about the victim, the more I understood the emotional tapestry of the town. It was a place where family secrets festered, where the past refused to stay buried. I felt an invisible thread binding me to the case, a connection that was both exhilarating and terrifying. I was not just investigating a crime; I was confronting the ghosts of my own history, searching for redemption in the darkest corners of my mind.

Late at night, when the world was quiet, the voices would come to me in dreams—soft whispers, urgent pleas for justice. They urged me to listen, to acknowledge the pain that had been silenced for too long. In those moments, I understood that the case was not merely about solving a murder; it was about healing, for both the town and myself. I began to see the importance of empathy, the necessity of understanding the stories behind the headlines, and the profound impact they had on everyone involved.

As I pieced together the fragments of the past, I realized that the truth was often more complicated than it seemed. Each revelation brought with it a new layer of complexity, intertwining my fate with that of the town. The voices from beyond were guiding me, urging me to confront my own demons as I sought to bring closure to those who had suffered. I was determined not to let their stories fade away, for in each whisper lay the heart of a mystery that demanded to be told, echoing long after the last page was turned.

Chapter 6: Crime Scene Analysis

The Clues Left Behind

The night felt heavy with secrets as I walked through the quiet streets of my small town, each shadow whispering of mysteries yet untold. The case that had haunted me for years was not just a distant memory; it was a living entity, breathing down my neck and urging me to uncover the truth. Each step echoed with the burden of the past, reminding me that the clues left behind were more than just breadcrumbs—they were pieces of a puzzle that I had yet to solve.

As I revisited the scene of the crime, the air was thick with the scent of damp earth, and memories flooded my mind. I could still see the outlines of the chalk marks where the investigators had stood, their faces etched with determination. Those markers had long faded, but the emotional scars remained fresh. I had spent countless nights replaying that day in my head, searching for something—anything—that would lead me to the answers I so desperately sought.

The first clue I found was a small, almost insignificant item hidden beneath the floorboards of my childhood home. It was a silver locket, tarnished with age, yet it shimmered with the weight of untold stories. I could feel the heartbeat of the past as I held it in my palm, sensing that it belonged to someone connected to the case. It was a reminder that every object, no matter how trivial, could hold the key to unraveling the tangled web of family secrets that had ensnared us all.

I reached out to the few who still lived in the town, hoping to piece together fragments of memories that time had obscured. With each conversation, I unearthed more clues, revealing a tapestry of lives intertwined with mine. The chilling realization dawned on me that the case wasn't just about the crime; it was about understanding how deeply our lives were affected by the past. Every whisper in the dark felt like a nudge from the universe, pushing me closer to the truth.

In my quest for answers, I discovered that the clues were not merely physical remnants of the past but emotional echoes that reverberated through generations. Each revelation brought me closer to confronting the shadows that had followed me home, reminding me that the journey to uncover the truth was as haunting as the mystery itself. It was a path fraught with danger and revelation, one that would ultimately lead me to the heart of the darkness that had long overshadowed my life.

The Science of the Unknown

In the quiet town of Willow Creek, the air was thick with secrets, each corner whispering tales of the past that refused to remain buried. The science of the unknown was not just a field of study; it was an entanglement of emotions, memories, and the inescapable echo of unresolved cases that haunted its residents. As the protagonist delved deeper into the cold case that had followed her home, she found herself grappling with more than just facts and figures; she was confronting the ghosts of her own past, intertwined with the mystery that loomed over her.

Psychological thrillers often hinge on the delicate balance between the mind and its dark corners. The protagonist's journey into the depths of this enigma was marked by moments of clarity and confusion, where the lines between reality and the supernatural blurred. Each clue she uncovered was a piece of her own history, revealing how personal traumas could distort perceptions and drive one toward the brink of madness. The science behind the unknown was not merely about solving a crime but understanding the psyche that fueled it.

As she partnered with a seasoned detective, the two formed a dynamic duo, navigating through the labyrinth of family secrets and small-town lies. Their investigation revealed that the past was not just a backdrop but a living entity that shaped their present. With each breakthrough, they unearthed not only the truth about the case but also the hidden facets of their own identities. This exploration of the psyche was as crucial as any forensic analysis, suggesting that the heart of every mystery lay in the emotional scars we carry.

The deeper they ventured, the more they realized that some truths were too painful to confront. The science of the unknown became a poignant metaphor for the barriers people erect to shield themselves from hurt. As the protagonist confronted her fears, she discovered that understanding the unknown was less about finding answers and more about embracing the complexities of human emotions. The haunting melodies of the past merged with the present, creating a symphony of unresolved issues that demanded attention.

In the end, the case that haunted her was not just about crime; it was about connection, healing, and the relentless pursuit of understanding oneself amidst chaos. The unknown was not something to be feared but explored, revealing layers of complexity that resonated deeply with her. In a world where shadows lingered and secrets thrived, the protagonist learned that sometimes, the most profound mysteries lie within, waiting to be unearthed through the brave act of facing the unknown head-on.

Chapter 7: Family Ties and Lies

Uncovering Hidden Truths

As I delved deeper into the case that had haunted me for years, I found myself facing the unsettling truth that the past was not as buried as I had once believed. Each new piece of evidence felt like a ghost from my past, whispering secrets only I could hear. The small town where I had grown up seemed to hold its breath, as if waiting for the revelations that were about to unfold. With the weight of unresolved feelings and memories pressing down on me, I knew that this wasn't just a mystery; it was a deeply personal journey into the shadows of my own history.

I began to uncover the hidden truths that had been obscured by time and silence. The more I investigated, the more I realized that the case was intertwined with my own family's secrets. Each interview with townsfolk revealed layers of deceit and betrayal that had festered beneath the surface. Their guarded responses served as a reminder that some truths are too painful to confront, and yet, the urgency to unveil them propelled me forward.

My partner in this quest, a seasoned detective with a keen intuition, helped me navigate the murky waters of this investigation. Together, we pieced together fragments of memories and evidence that revealed a tapestry of connections I had never anticipated. Each discovery felt like a step closer to not only solving the case but also understanding my own complicated ties to the past. The thrill of the chase was intoxicating, but the emotional toll was heavy, as I wrestled with the ghosts of my childhood.

As we reopened the cold case, I began to confront the demons that had followed me home. The unsettling realization that my own life was intricately linked to the mystery was both frightening and exhilarating. Each revelation brought to light not only the dark corners of the town but also the shadows lurking within my own heart. I was no longer just an amateur sleuth; I was a participant in a narrative that demanded resolution.

Ultimately, uncovering these hidden truths was about more than just solving a mystery. It was a journey toward healing, understanding, and reclaiming my identity. The case that had haunted me for so long became a catalyst for transformation, challenging me to face the uncomfortable realities of my past. As the pieces fell into place, I learned that sometimes the most profound discoveries are not just about the truth of others, but about the truths we hold within ourselves.

The Burden of Secrets

Secrets have a way of weaving themselves into the very fabric of our lives, often shaping our decisions and altering our perceptions. For Clara, the protagonist of this psychological thriller, the burden of secrets was not just a personal struggle but a haunting presence that seemed to follow her every move. Living in a small town, where whispers travel faster than light, she felt the weight of unspoken truths pressing down on her, suffocating her spirit and clouding her judgment. Each day that passed felt like a reminder of what was hidden beneath the surface, a constant battle between the need to uncover the truth and the fear of what might be revealed.

As Clara delved deeper into the cold case that had haunted her community for decades, she found herself grappling with her own buried secrets. The investigation unearthed memories that she thought she had buried long ago, intertwining her personal history with the mystery at hand. Every clue she uncovered was a thread that pulled her back into her past, challenging her to confront the shadows that loomed over her. The deeper she went, the more she realized that the burden of secrets was not just a theme of the case; it was her own emotional entanglement that made the truth seem both enticing and terrifying.

The town itself seemed to hold its breath as Clara navigated through whispers and half-truths. Her journey revealed the complexities of human relationships, where loyalty often clashed with the desire for honesty. Clara discovered that many residents harbored their own secrets, and as she pieced together the story, she realized that the true mystery was not just the crime itself but the interconnected lives of those involved. Each revelation felt like a weight lifted, yet another secret would replace it, leaving her feeling as if she were carrying an invisible load that threatened to crush her under its pressure.

The haunting nature of secrets became evident as Clara encountered those who had been deeply affected by the unresolved case. Their stories echoed her own struggles and fears, creating a web of emotional connections that were impossible to untangle. With every conversation, she felt the lines between her past and the present blur, as if the ghosts of those secrets were reaching out to her. This connection deepened her resolve, compelling her to not only seek justice for the victim but also to find closure for herself.

Ultimately, "The Burden of Secrets" serves as a poignant reminder that the truth can be both liberating and devastating. Clara's journey through the labyrinth of her own secrets and those of others illustrates the profound impact that hidden truths can have on our lives. In a world where silence often hides the most significant stories, Clara learns that facing the burdens of the past is the only way to move forward, and that sometimes, the secrets we keep can define us in ways we never expected.

Chapter 8: The Turning Point

Confronting the Past

As the sun dipped below the horizon, casting long shadows across the small town of Willow Creek, Maria felt the weight of her past pressing down on her. The unsolved case that haunted her wasn't just a distant memory; it was a ghost that lingered, echoing through the hallways of her mind. Each step she took toward the old police station felt like a confrontation with her own fears and regrets. The case that had once consumed her life was now a thread that pulled her back into the depths of what she thought she had left behind.

Maria's heart raced as she entered the station, the familiar scent of old paper and worn leather filling her senses. Memories flooded back as she recalled the late nights spent poring over files, desperately seeking answers to questions that had no easy solutions. Her hands trembled slightly as she reached for the case file, its pages yellowed with age, a testament to the time that had passed since the last investigation. This was not just a case; it was a personal journey, intertwined with her own identity and the secrets she had tried to bury.

The deeper she delved into the details of the case, the more she uncovered about the town's dark history. Secrets lay buried beneath the surface, waiting to be unearthed. Each revelation felt like a piece of a puzzle that had been scattered across years, and with every piece she fit together, the haunting memories of her own past began to resurface. The townspeople, once familiar faces, began to morph into suspects, each with their own hidden agendas and stories to tell.

As Maria pieced together the narrative, she couldn't help but reflect on her own life choices. The ghosts of her past weren't just remnants of the case; they were intertwined with her relationships and the decisions that had led her to this moment. Confronting the past meant facing the uncomfortable truths about herself, her family, and the web of lies that had ensnared her for so long. The investigation was no longer just about solving a mystery; it was about reclaiming her identity and finding closure.

In the end, confronting the past became a cathartic experience for Maria. Each discovery brought her closer to not only solving the case but also healing the wounds that had festered within her. The shadows of Willow Creek whispered their secrets, and as she embraced the truth, she realized that the only way to move forward was to confront what had once haunted her. The case that had followed her home was a reminder that the past, no matter how painful, could ultimately lead to redemption and self-discovery.

A Dangerous Encounter

The air was thick with tension as I found myself standing at the edge of the old, decrepit house. This was the place where it all began—the unsolved mystery that had haunted my dreams. I could feel the weight of the past pressing down on me, the memories of whispers and shadows intertwining with the present. With each step, I could almost hear the echoes of laughter that once filled this space, now replaced by an eerie silence that made my skin crawl.

As I approached the front door, a chill ran down my spine. It was like stepping into another world, one where time had stopped and secrets lay hidden beneath layers of dust. I hesitated, recalling the warnings I had received about this place. They said it was cursed, that those who dared to enter would leave with more than they came with. But I was drawn here, driven by an insatiable need to uncover the truth that had eluded me for so long.

The moment I crossed the threshold, a sense of foreboding washed over me. The dim light filtered through cracked windows, illuminating the remnants of a life once lived. I could feel eyes watching me, though I was alone—or so I thought. The air crackled with energy, and I sensed the presence of something beyond the physical realm. It was as if the house itself was alive, holding onto its secrets and daring me to pry them loose.

As I navigated the narrow hallways, flashes of memories assaulted me—laughter, anger, sorrow. I stumbled upon a room filled with old photographs, each one telling a story of love and loss. But amidst the nostalgia, there was something darker lurking in the shadows. A sudden noise startled me, and I spun around, heart racing. I wasn't alone anymore; the danger I had been warned about was very real, and it was closing in.

In that moment, I realized that this was not just a journey into the past but a confrontation with my own demons. The case that had haunted me for years was intertwined with the very walls that surrounded me. I had come seeking answers, but what I found was far more complicated—a dangerous encounter with the truth that would change everything I thought I knew about myself and the world around me.

Chapter 9: The Unraveling

Piecing It All Together

As the pieces of the case began to come together, I felt an unsettling familiarity gnawing at the edges of my mind. The small town where I had grown up was not just a backdrop; it was a character in its own right, with secrets woven into its fabric. Each interview I conducted brought back memories—faces from my childhood, whispers of rumors long buried. The haunting nature of this investigation was not merely about solving a mystery; it was about confronting my own past, entwined with the lives of those I had once known.

Delving deeper into the lives of the victims, I uncovered family secrets that were devastating yet illuminating. It seemed everyone had something to hide, from hidden affairs to long-held grudges, each revelation pulling me further into a spiral of emotional complexity. The local diner, once a place of comfort, now felt like a trap filled with echoes of laughter and pain. I found myself questioning not just their motives, but my own—what connections had I overlooked in my pursuit of the truth?

The chilling feeling of being watched became a constant companion. It was as though the unresolved tensions of the past had come alive, shadowing my every move. I started to notice patterns linking the victims to my own family, hints of a darkness that had seeped into our lives without anyone noticing. The more I pieced together, the more I realized that this investigation was as much about the town's history as it was about the present. The line between the two blurred, and I couldn't help but wonder if I was meant to uncover these truths or if they were better left buried.

Each clue felt like an invitation to confront my fears, urging me to face the ghosts that had haunted me for years. With each breakthrough, I felt the weight of responsibility settle on my shoulders. The stakes were higher than I had anticipated, and the emotional toll was beginning to show. I was no longer just an amateur sleuth; I was a participant in a narrative that had been unfolding long before I had entered the scene. The realization that my own life was intertwined with the mystery was both terrifying and exhilarating.

Ultimately, piecing it all together was not just about solving the case; it was about understanding myself and the legacy of the town I had thought I knew. The threads I uncovered wove a tapestry of pain, resilience, and unexpected connections. My journey had become a haunting exploration of what it means to confront the past, and as I stood on the precipice of discovery, I knew that some secrets would forever shape my identity, binding me to the case that had indeed followed me home.

The Final Revelation

The air was thick with tension as I stood in the dimly lit room, the shadows whispering secrets of a past that refused to stay buried. The final revelation was upon me, and with it came a chilling realization that the case I thought I had solved was merely the surface of something much deeper and more sinister. Each clue I had pieced together now felt like a breadcrumb leading me back to my own haunted memories, connecting my fate with that of the victims in ways I never anticipated.

As I sifted through the remnants of the investigation, the faces of the lost echoed in my mind, their stories intertwining with my own. I could feel their pain, their unresolved issues, and their desperate need for closure. The psychological weight of this case pressed heavily on my chest, igniting a fire within me to uncover the truth—not just for them, but for myself. I realized that this was more than a mystery; it was a personal battle with the shadows of my past that had followed me home.

The small town, with its picturesque facade, hid dark secrets beneath its charm. I found myself retracing my steps through familiar streets, each corner holding memories that now felt tainted. I approached the people I once trusted, only to discover that their loyalties were as fragile as the fragile alliances I had formed. The bond I thought I had with my fellow sleuth was tested, revealing fractures that paralleled the case itself. Trust, I learned, was as elusive as the truth.

With each new piece of evidence, the web of deception became more intricate, ensnaring me in its grip. The familial ties that bound the victims to my own life were unraveling, exposing a chilling connection that felt predestined. I was no longer just an amateur sleuth; I had become an unwilling participant in a psychological game that had no clear end. The stakes were high, and as the final revelation loomed closer, I knew I had to confront my own demons to find the resolution that eluded us all.

In the end, it was not just about solving a case; it was about understanding the depths of human emotion and the complexity of our connections. The final revelation forced me to confront the shadows that had haunted me for too long, leading to a catharsis that was both liberating and terrifying. I emerged from the darkness, forever changed, realizing that some cases never truly end—they linger, intertwining with our lives in ways that challenge our very understanding of justice and closure.

Chapter 10: Closure or Continuation?

The Aftermath

The aftermath of the case settled heavily on my shoulders like a shroud that refused to lift. Each day, as I walked through the familiar streets of our small town, I felt the whispers of the past echoing through the air. The unresolved questions gnawed at me, haunting my thoughts and casting shadows over the bright faces of my neighbors. I had thought that solving the mystery would bring closure, but instead, it opened a door to deeper, darker secrets that intertwined with my own life.

Every interaction became tinged with suspicion, as if the very air I breathed was laced with the remnants of betrayal and despair. Friends turned into strangers, and I found myself questioning the motives of those I once trusted. The case that had captivated the town now felt like an invisible chain, binding me to a truth I was not ready to confront. I frequently replayed the details in my mind, searching for clues that might lead to a resolution, yet every avenue seemed to spiral back to me.

The nights were the hardest, filled with an unsettling silence that echoed the chaos of my thoughts. I often dreamt of the faces involved, their expressions twisted in anguish and desperation. It was as if they were reaching out to me from the shadows, imploring me to find justice for their suffering. I realized then that this case was not just about the crime itself; it was about the emotional scars it left behind, shaping the very fabric of my existence.

As I delved deeper into the lives affected by the case, I discovered connections that entwined our fates in ways I had never anticipated. Each revelation peeled back layers of my own life, forcing me to confront the family secrets I had tucked away for years. The haunting realization that I was not just an observer but a participant in this psychological thriller sent chills down my spine. I was drawn into a web of intrigue that blurred the lines between right and wrong, challenging everything I thought I knew.

In the end, the aftermath was not just about solving a mystery; it was about understanding the complexities of the human psyche. The case that had followed me home had become a mirror reflecting my own fears and desires. As I stood at the crossroads of my past and present, I knew that the journey was far from over. With each step I took, I embraced the haunting echoes of the case, ready to face the truths that lay in wait, knowing they would forever alter my path.

Echoes of the Past

The past has a way of weaving itself into the present, echoing through the corridors of our minds and hearts. For Maria, the protagonist in "The Case That Haunted Me," those echoes were not merely whispers; they were thunderous roars that threatened to engulf her. As she navigated the small town of Willow Creek, memories of a tragic cold case resurfaced, intertwining with her own life in ways she could never have anticipated. Each step forward felt like a step backward, as the shadows of lost lives loomed ever closer.

Maria found herself drawn to the remnants of the case that had haunted her family for decades, a mystery that was as deeply personal as it was perplexing. The unresolved questions echoed in her mind like a haunting melody, stirring a sense of duty to uncover the truth. With each new piece of evidence she uncovered, she felt a part of herself reconnecting to the past, as if the lives lost were calling out to her for justice. This emotional entanglement began to blur the lines between her own reality and the ghosts of the past.

As she delved deeper, the small town's secrets began to unravel, revealing connections she never expected. The townsfolk, with their guarded expressions, held the keys to the mystery; their reluctance spoke volumes about the pain that lingered in the air. Sarah's amateur sleuthing took her through a tangled web of family secrets, where trust was a luxury and betrayal was common currency. The more she learned, the more she understood that some echoes were meant to be silenced, and others were desperate to be heard.

The psychological toll of her investigation weighed heavily on Maria. Each revelation was met with a haunting sense of déjà vu, as if she were not just a bystander in this story, but an integral part of it. The case did not just follow her home; it became a dark companion, entwining itself with her thoughts and dreams. With every sleepless night, she grappled with the ghosts of the unresolved, feeling their pain as acutely as her own. In this psychological thriller, the past was not merely a backdrop but a living entity that shaped her very existence.

Ultimately, Maria's journey became one of self-discovery, as she battled not only the mysteries of Willow Creek but the shadows within her own soul. In seeking to understand the echoes of the past, she uncovered truths about herself that she had long buried. The case that haunted her became a catalyst for change, forcing her to confront her fears and embrace the complexity of her emotions. As the echoes faded, a new understanding emerged, illuminating the path forward, forever changing her life in ways she had never imagined. It's a beautiful day.

Author Richard Trillion Mantey

Author Biography

Richard Trillion Mantey is a master of psychological storytelling—an author whose words do more than entertain; they awaken, challenge, and transform.

Known for crafting emotionally charged narratives that explore the hidden corridors of the human mind, Richard's work blends suspense, introspection, and raw psychological truth. His stories are not just about what happens on the surface—but about what lingers beneath: the unspoken fears, the buried memories, and the silent battles we all face.

Drawing inspiration from human behavior, trauma, resilience, and the power of perception, Richard writes with a rare intensity that pulls readers into deeply immersive worlds. His storytelling is both cinematic and intimate—where every character feels real, every moment feels lived, and every twist cuts deep.

But beyond the thrill, his mission is clear:

To remind readers that the mind is powerful…

Memory is fragile…

And truth is never as simple as it seems.

Through The Case That Haunted Me, Richard invites readers into a haunting journey—not just through a mystery, but through the psychological echoes that shape who we become.

His voice is bold. His message is timeless.

And his stories stay with you… long after the final page.